For John and the six moggies – Linda
For R.J.P. with love – Rhian

Published in 1993 by Magi Publications
in association with Star Books International, 55 Crowland Avenue, Hayes, Middx UB3 4JP
Text © 1993 by Linda Jennings
Illustrations © 1993 by Rhian Nest James
Typeset by Calvert's Press, London
Printed and bound in Belgium by Proost N.V. Turnhout
ISBN 1 85430 253 1

Magi Publications, London

Scramcat

Written by
Linda Jennings

Illustrated by
Rhian Nest James

Scramcat had one torn ear and a look on his face that said, "Watch out, or I'll push your face in."

Everyone had pushed Scramcat around since he was a kitten. Since he had been thrown away with the Christmas wrapping paper, he had had to fight to survive.

"SCRAM, CAT!" shouted Mrs Wilkins when the big tom tried to steal the Sunday joint.

"SCRAM, CAT!" yelled the owners of a slinky Siamese who Scramcat confronted on the lawn. His tail was bushy with aggression, his eyes round as Belisha beacons.

"SCRAM, CAT!" cried Trish Allen
from No. 6, as Scramcat tried to climb
the bird-table.

Nobody loved Scramcat. Nobody fed him, not even the old bag-lady who brought food for all the strays. "SCRAM, CAT!" she shouted. "You greedy thing, you." She always shooed him away, because he had once fought another cat over a chicken leg and scratched its nose.

One day Scramcat noticed an open window at No. 9.
He leapt lightly onto the sill and looked into an empty
room. There was a comfortable-looking armchair in the
corner, and comfort was not something Scramcat enjoyed
very often. He ran across the room, padded several times
on the cushion, and purring softly, curled himself into a
tight ball.

Scramcat had not noticed other feet following his through the window. They leapt softly into the room too, and tiptoed over to the mantelpiece, ignoring the sleeping furry cushion on the pink armchair. Two hands greedily grasped a row of silver cups and slid them into an open holdall. A silver inkstand followed the cups, then a delicately carved elephant.

Suddenly the window slammed shut. Scramcat woke up, and he saw the man. Scramcat didn't hang around. He shot out of the chair, and ran towards the open door . . .

. . . just as the man was heading in the same direction.
"Aagh!" he yelled, as he tripped over Scramcat and came
crashing down. He was too badly hurt to yell "Scram, cat".

But Mrs Freemantle, who lived at No. 9, was just coming
in through the front door.
"SCRAM, C . . . !" she began, and then she noticed the
man on the floor. He was sitting up, clutching his leg.
"I think it's broken," he said.

Scramcat ran out of the door and dived into the bushes
by the front gate. He had left a lot of hairs and a few
fleas on the lovely pink chair – he would never dare go
into that house again. As he lay there, trembling from
head to foot, a white car with flashing blue lights drew
up at the gate.

Two blue-uniformed men got out, and Scramcat watched as they went up to the house, and returned with the man he had tripped up. The man was hopping on one leg. They all climbed into the car and it drove away.

"Come puss, come puss!" Scramcat pricked up his ears. He saw Mrs Freemantle standing in the garden with a white saucer.

Scramcat could smell raw mince.
"It must be a trap," he thought. "No one would
offer me *food*."

Scramcat crawled cautiously from the bushes.
Mrs Freemantle was still standing there. For a moment
both cat and woman looked at each other, and they saw
loneliness. Very cautiously, Scramcat crept across the
lawn towards the saucer. He ate and he ate, until
he'd licked the saucer clean.

Now every morning and every evening Mrs Freemantle is there with a saucer of fresh food for Scramcat. But of course he isn't called Scramcat anymore.

"Come puss, come puss," calls Mrs Freemantle, and the big tom shyly pads up to his friend, enjoying his new name.